WORDS AND ART

Laura Ljungkvist

Follow the Line to School

Viking

An Imprint of Penguin Group (USA) Inc.

SCHOOL

is starting, how exciting.
Music, reading,
math, and writing.

Lunchtime, recess, art,
and more.
Follow the line
and let's

EXPLORE

Say hello!

HELLO!

HELLO

to your friends

and GO to your classroom.

Fred is the class pet. Can you guess what kind of animal he is?

Look at the alphabet chart. What letter does your name start with?

What sport would you play with the ball in this room?

red

orange

yellow

green

blue

purple

September

Monday

A B C D E F
G H I J K L M
N O P Q R S T
U V W X Y Z

good morning
science
library
art
free play
lunch
recess
math
music
show-and-tell
good-bye

CARING FOR FRED:
fresh water
food
clean cage
cuddles

WELCOME

Follow the line to the science corner...

to learn about

ANIMALS

and the different places they live in the

WORLD

Elephants live in Africa and Asia. How many elephants do you see?

Many chickens live on farms. What other animals here might live on a farm?

Whales live in the ocean. What other animals shown here also live in the water?

leaves

shells

bugs

rocks

Follow the line to the library . . .

to pick out a

BOOK

and to hear a

STORY

Paul Province

Ljungkvist

Bob Bridge

Santana

Ljungkvist ★ ★ Once Upon a Line

GUSTAVO

Ljungkvist

Life Line

A Dog Named Taxi

My Cousin Sonja

SAM ARENA ⚾ HOME RUN

Ljungkvist | Line Up

Emma Jonsson | A Long Time Ago

Piglet Party ⦿ Patsy Pine

There is an open book on the chair. What do you think it is about?

How many headsets do you see for the listening station?

Which book on this page do you think is about baseball?

A Dog Named Taxi
Paul Province

My Cousin Sonja
Sarah Santana

A Long Time Ago
Emma Jonsson

LISTEN

Follow the line to the art room . . .

to **PAINT**

draw, and **CREATE**

What color do you get if you mix blue and yellow paint?

Which pictures on the wall are made from cut paper?

There is a paintbrush in a cup of water on the table. What color paint was on the brush?

beads

ribbon

felt

string

teacher

Follow the line back to your classroom . . .

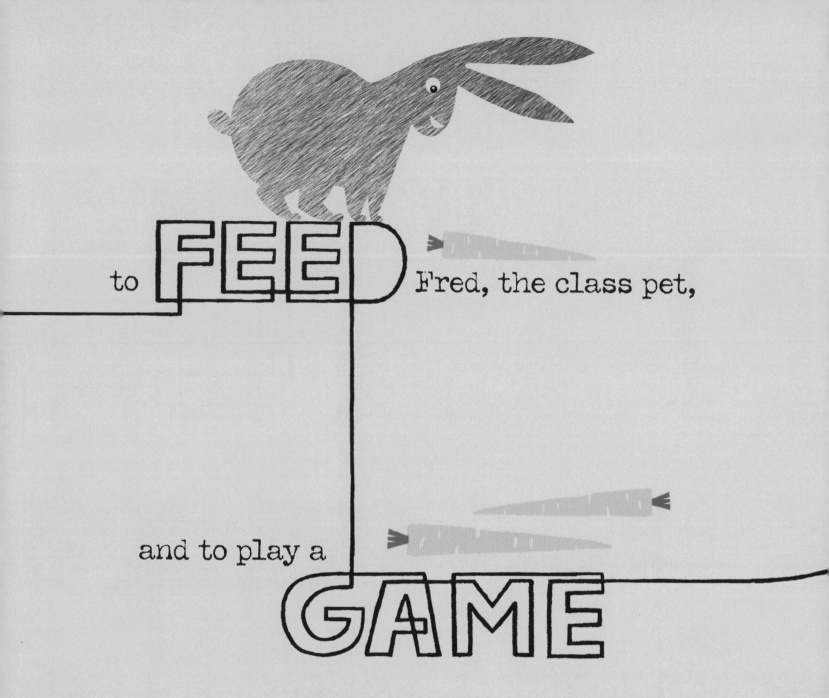

to **FEED** Fred, the class pet,

and to play a **GAME**

What would you feed to Fred?

Using your finger, can you find your way to the star at the center of the maze?

What number did the spinner land on?

Follow the line
to the cafeteria . . .

to eat your

LUNCH

Don't forget to

WASH your hands first.

What fruits do you see here?

Which of the foods shown here would you pack in your own lunch box?

How many types of pasta can you count?

Follow the line to the playground . . .

to **RUN**

and play
at

RECESS

Someone left a baseball cap outside. Can you find it?

How many balls do you see?

What colors are the jump ropes?

Follow the line to the math area . . .

to learn about

COUNTING

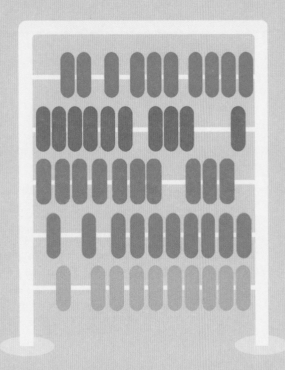

and

SHAPES

One number is missing from the puzzle on the table. Can you find it?

If you are counting by twos, which number comes after six?

How many triangular blocks do you see on the table?

counting
by tens → 10 20 30 40 50 60 70 80 90 100

counting by twos

2 4 6 8 10

ways to make ten

0 + 10 = 10
1 + 9 = 10
2 + 8 = 10
3 + 7 = 10
4 + 6 = 10
5 + 5 = 10

tell time!

weights

blocks

rulers

flash cards

1 2 3 4 5 6

Follow the line to the music room . . .

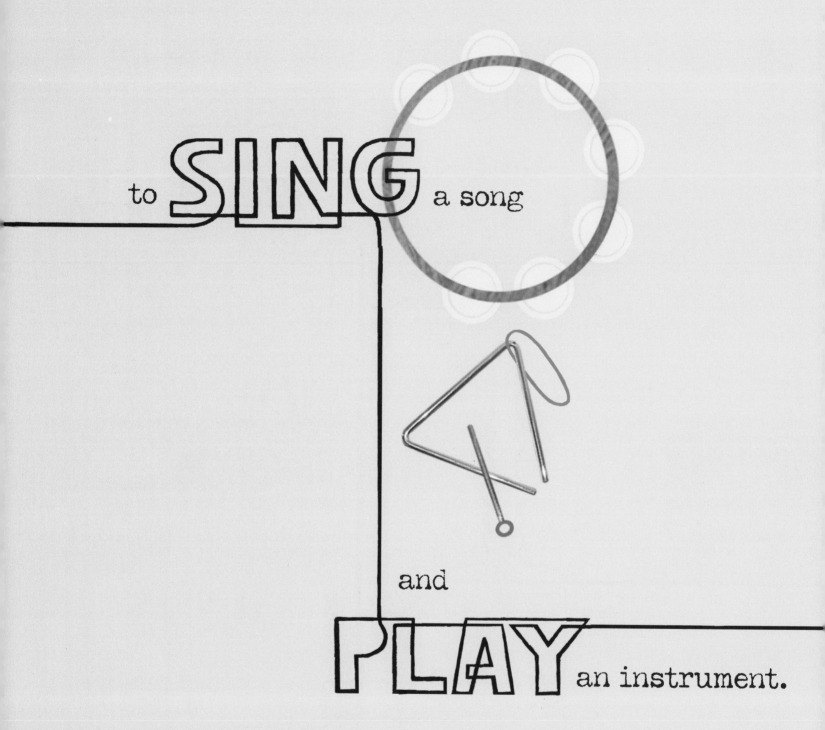

to **SING** a song

and

PLAY an instrument.

Which of these instruments do you blow into?

How many instruments shown here have strings?

Which of these instruments would you shake and rattle?

Follow the line back to your classroom . . .

because it's time for

SHOW

and

TELL

Someone brought in a seashell collection. How many shells can you count?

Which of these things are gold?

How many animals do you see?

Follow the line out the door,
because it's time to go . . .

HOME!

It's so much fun

to learn

new

THINGS

EXIT

I wonder what . . .

TOMORROW brings.